This igloo book
belongs to:

....

igloobooks

Published in 2022
First published in the UK by Igloo Books Ltd
An imprint of Igloo Books Ltd
Cottage Farm, NN6 0BJ, UK
Owned by Bonnier Books
Sveavägen 56, Stockholm, Sweden
www.igloobooks.com

1122 002
2 4 6 8 10 9 7 5 3
ISBN 978-1-80022-676-0

Written by Sienna Williams
Illustrated by Julia Seal

Designed by Alex Alexandrou
Edited by Stephanie Moss

Printed and manufactured in China

All We Need Is
LOVE

igloobooks

What if each morning, you shouted, "SURPRISE!"

... and gave me ten gifts
when I opened my eyes?

Or, we moved to a magical palace one day? I'd fill it with toys so my friends could all play!

Maybe a fabulous feast would be fun?

With cream cakes and doughnuts
and sweet sticky buns!

That trip of a lifetime.
At last, we could go!

Splish-splash
in the sea...

... or swish-swish in the snow.

If we went shopping
as much as we liked...

... we'd buy and we'd spend, every day and all night!

You'd throw
me a party
that went on
till three.

Guests could come all round the world, just for me!

Even with riches and gold like a king...

... I'd know that none of it meant **ANYTHING.**

So, don't bring me the moon or the twinkling stars.

To show me you love me, you needn't go far.

For even if marching bands played to the beat...

... at parades in my honour right here on our street...

... nothing and no one could EVER compare to anyone, anything or anywhere,

as much as YOUR LOVE

and just knowing you...

... CARE.

So, I don't need presents. No, not even yours!
All we need is LOVE. Not anything more.